# Chicks Just Want to Have Fun

You can read more stories about
the animals from Potter's Barn
by collecting the rest of the series.

For a complete list, look at
the back of the book.

# Chicks Just Want to Have Fun

### Francesca Simon

#### Illustrated by Emily Bolam

Orion
Children's Books

For Jenny Glencross

Far Away Field

Cross-Patch Meadow

Snapdragon Pond

Silver Meadow

Butterfly Field

Muddy Pond

N
W
E
S

Big Woods

Thistle Meadow Old Barn

POTTER'S
~BARN~

Orchard

# Hello from everyone

Henny-Penny

Cluck
Cluck

The chicks

Cheep
Cheep

Squeaky the cat

Miaow

Moooo

Daffodil the cow

Rosie the calf

Father Goat

Bleat

Billy the Kid

Mother Sheep

Baaaaa

Tilly and Tam
the lambs

Mother Duck

Quack
Quack

Five Ducklings

Neigh

Trot the horse

Honk Honk

Gabby Goose

Woof

Buster the dog

Oink oink

Belle the pig

Cock-a-doodle-doo!

Red Rooster

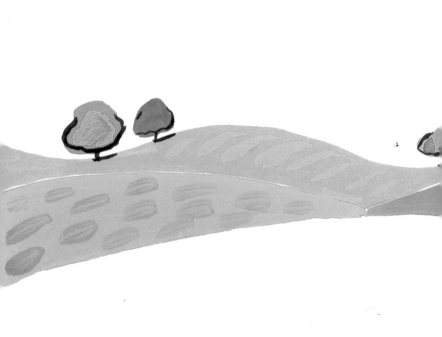

# Welcome to Potter's Barn!

The sun always shines and the fun never stops at Potter's Barn Farm. Join the animals on their adventures as they sing, stomp, make cakes, get lost, run off, and go wild.

Henny-Penny was tucking
her chicks in for the night.

"It's not fair," cheeped the chicks.
"It's not even dark yet. Why do
we have to go to bed so early?"

"Because you're young
and you need your rest,"
said Henny-Penny.

"But we're not sleepy,"
said the chicks.

"You will be soon,"
said Henny-Penny.
"Now, no more chit-chat.
Goodnight, chicks.
Sleep tight."

And she closed
the hen house door.

For a moment there was silence.

"It's not fair!"
said the black speckled chick.

"I bet everyone else is up having fun,"
said the red chick.

"I bet Belle is dancing," said
the brown chick.

"I bet Billy the Kid is playing
football," said the yellow one.

"I bet Daffodil is having a party,"
said the fluffy white.

The chicks looked at each other.
"Let's go and find out,"
they cheeped.

And they sneaked out of the hen
house over to Belle's pen.

Belle was standing by the trough,
singing her favourite song
to her piglets.

A big fat pig

A big big fat pig

A big big big fat pig

A big big fat pig

A big fat pig

A pig

Pig

Oink

"Not much fun here,"
whispered the brown chick.
"Let's see what Billy the Kid
is up to."

Off they pitter-pattered.

Billy was in his shed
talking to himself.
"Thank you, yes, I will have
a fourth helping of those delicious
cardboard boxes," he said.

"Not much fun here,"
peeped the yellow chick.

"There must be a party
at the barn," said the
black speckled chick.

Off they fluttered.

A beam of light shone
under a small crack at the
bottom of the barn door.

"I hear voices," whispered
the yellow chick.
The chicks squeezed
underneath the door.

"Hi, everybody! We're here!
Let's party!" they cheeped.

Buster looked up
from his cushion.

Daffodil and Squeaky
stopped talking.

The ducks untucked their heads from under their wings.

Mother Sheep opened her eyes.

"What are you doing here so late, chicks?" asked Daffodil.

"We're looking for the party," they peeped.

"What party?" said Daffodil.

"The party you have when we're asleep," said the fluffy white chick.

"We're much too tired
to have a party,"
said Daffodil.

"So what are you doing?"
said the yellow chick.

"Just chatting,"
said Squeaky.

# "Boring!"
cheeped the chicks.

"Hurry home now, before
Henny-Penny finds you missing,"
said Daffodil.

The chicks filed sadly
out of the barn.

"Good night, everyone," they said,
and crept back into the hen house.

"There must be a party somewhere,"
said the brown chick.

"There is!" said the black speckled
chick. "Right here!"

"What's going on in there?"
called Henny-Penny.

"Nothing, Mum,"
said the chicks.

"We're just getting
sleepy."

Cheep cheep
follow me

Did you enjoy the
little chicks' story?
Can you remember the
things that happened?

Why don't the chicks want
to go to bed?

What does the red chick say
when Henny-Penny closes the
hen house door?

What does the fluffy white chick
think is happening while they're
tucked up in bed?

What is Belle the pig doing when the
chicks go to her pen?

Who else do the chicks visit?

What do the chicks think is happening at the barn?

What are the animals in the barn doing?

Where do the chicks find their party?

For more farmyard fun with the animals at Potter's Barn, look out for the other books in the series.

Runaway Duckling

Where Are my Lambs?

# Billy the Kid
# Goes Wild

# Barnyard
# Hullabaloo

## Mish Mash Hash

## Moo Baa Baa Quack